ANDY SHANE

and the
Barn Sale Mystery

ANDY SHANE
and the
Barn Sale Mystery

Jennifer Richard Jacobson

illustrated by Abby Carter

CANDLEWICK PRESS

For the teachers
J. R. J.

For my three brothers:
Ted, Mike, and Kip
A. C.

First edition 2009

Library of Congress Cataloging-in-Publication Data

Jacobson, Jennifer, date.
Andy Shane and the barn sale mystery / Jennifer Richard Jacobson ; illustrated by Abby Carter. —1st ed.
p. cm.
Summary: After Andy hosts a barn sale to raise money
for a case for Granny Webb's binoculars, he realizes that they accidentally were sold,
so with Dolores's help they try to track down the missing binoculars.

ISBN 978-0-7636-3599-2

[1. Lost and found possessions — Fiction. 2. Friendship — Fiction. 3. Mystery and detective stories.]
I. Carter, Abby, ill. II. Title.
PZ7.J1529Ac 2009
[E] — dc22   2008017974
2 4 6 8 10 9 7 5 3 1
Printed in the United States of America

This book was typeset in Vendome.
The illustrations were done in black pencil and black watercolor wash.

Candlewick Press
99 Dover Street
Somerville, Massachusetts 02144

visit us at www.candlewick.com

CONTENTS

Chapter 1   That's It!   *1*

Chapter 2   Big Barn Blunder   *13*

Chapter 3   Solving the Mystery   *25*

Chapter 4   Unbelievable   *43*

1

That's It!

Every year Andy Shane and Granny
Webb celebrated their unbirthdays.
They always chose a fall day when
the jam was made, the tomatoes
were canned, and the grass no longer
needed mowing. In other words—
the perfect time for a party.

This year, Andy wanted to give Granny the best present ever. So he sat down and made a list of all the things she loved:

Birds
Butterflies
Bugs
Bats

But he couldn't give her any of these things. Granny didn't want to collect living things; she just wanted to watch them. He added *Binoculars* to the list. Granny loved her binoculars.

Aha! That's it! Andy knew the perfect gift. He would buy a case to protect the binoculars when he and Granny went hiking through the woods!

That afternoon, Andy rode his

bike to Dolores Starbuckle's house.

"I've thought of the perfect present

to buy Granny Webb," he said.

"But your piggy bank is empty,"

said Dolores, who was very practical.

Andy had forgotten. He'd spent
all his money on marbles over the
summer. Dolores Starbuckle didn't
forget anything.

"I'll earn the money," said Andy.

"Doing what?" asked Dolores.

Andy wasn't sure, but he'd think
of something.

Later, Dolores and Andy were
walking Lucky Duck when they saw
an old chair sitting by the side of the
road. The chair had a sign that said,
FREE. TAKE ME.

"Wow," said Dolores. "You could give Granny Webb this chair!"

"What would she want with an old chair?" asked Andy.

"You could fix it up—"

"And sell it!" said Andy. "That's it! I can have a barn sale!"

"I'll help!" said Dolores.

FREE
TAKE
ME

So Andy got his wagon, and he
and Dolores walked up and down
the streets in their neighborhood,
collecting old plates and lampshades,
mops and muffin tins.

"Why, Andy Shane," said Granny Webb. "What are you doing with all these things?"

"We're having a barn sale!" shouted Dolores.

Granny could not believe the piles and piles and piles of things taking up the space in her barn. She collapsed into the chair with the FREE sign. "I'll help," she said.

Andy, Dolores, and Granny made posters to hang around town. They decorated flyers and put them up at the post office, in the barber shop, and at the grocery store. Granny even helped Andy and Dolores put an ad in the newspaper.

2

Big Barn Blunder

On the day of the sale, people began

lining up outside the barn even

before Andy had set up a table with

a money jar.

When everything was ready, Dolores opened the doors and people rushed in. They couldn't wait to buy hats and rakes, water wings and pillows.

While parents raced around the barn looking for bargains, children hugged and petted Lucky Duck. He gave kisses for free.

Andy and Dolores helped people find the very objects they were looking for. They counted money and made change.

When visitors learned about Granny's apple orchard, she offered to give them a tour.

"Wow," said Andy, looking around. "We've sold almost everything!"

"Yup," said Dolores, holding up a sweater with the alphabet on it. "The lady who bought the binoculars wanted this sweater, but it wasn't her size."

"Binoculars?" asked Andy.

"You know," said Dolores. "The ones that were hanging on the wall."

"Those weren't for sale!" said Andy. "Those were Granny's binoculars. She loved those!"

"How was I supposed to know that?" asked Dolores.

"They didn't have a price tag," said Andy.

"I thought we forgot to give them a price tag," said Dolores.

"I was going to buy her a case for her unbirthday," said Andy.

"But you didn't tell *me*, Andy Shane!"

It was true. He hadn't told her.

What would Granny say when
she discovered they had sold
her binoculars? She would be so
disappointed!

Dolores seemed to read his mind. "Well, Andy," she said, "we'll just have to get them back."

Dolores tried to remember everything she could about the woman who bought the binoculars. "Make a list, Andy," she said.

Andy got out his notebook and wrote:

1.) Bought lots of children's books and crayons

2.) Had bright red marker on her hands

3.) Hummed the words to "The Wheels on the Bus"

"Maybe she's a librarian," said Dolores. "She did buy a lot of books."

"Or," said Andy, remembering the alphabet sweater, "a teacher!"

3
Solving the Mystery

Andy and Dolores decided that she
must be the new nursery school
teacher at the Little Red Schoolhouse.
That afternoon they rode their bikes
down to the school to investigate. But
because it was Saturday, the building
was locked.

"*Now* what are we going to do?"
asked Andy.

"Maybe the binoculars are inside,"
said Dolores.

"I could look in the windows if
they weren't so high," said Andy.

"Here," said Dolores, cupping her
hands. "I'll give you a boost."

Andy stood on Dolores's hands
and peeked in the schoolhouse
window.

"There's a woman in there!"

"Let me see!" said Dolores, dropping Andy to the ground.

Andy cupped his hands and lifted Dolores into the air. "That's her!" said Dolores. She banged on the windowpane.

The woman came outside. "You're the children who had the barn sale," she said.

"You bought the binoculars," said Dolores.

"But they weren't really for sale,"

said Andy. "They belong to my

Granny Webb."

"Oh, dear," said the woman. "I met a man while I was walking to my car who offered to buy the binoculars from me."

"Did you sell them?" asked Andy Shane.

"I did," said the woman. "I don't know the man's name, but let me tell you everything I remember about him."

Andy pulled out his notebook and made a new list:

"It's Mr. Merry, the baker!"

shouted Andy and Dolores together.

They thanked the teacher and

rode to one of their favorite places:

the Merry Muffin Bakery.

"Hello, you two," the baker said. "I was just using my new cookie cutters!"

"Did you buy a pair of binoculars?" asked Andy.

"From the teacher?" Dolores added.

"Because they belong to my Granny Webb," said Andy Shane.

"Oh," said Mr. Merry. "I just made a trade with the antique dealer next door. He had a rare cookbook I wanted."

"So now *he* has the binoculars?" asked Andy.

"I'm afraid so," said the baker.

Dolores and Andy walked into the dimly lit shop. There were the binoculars, sitting on a table. And right beside the binoculars was a case. Andy looked at the price tags. Even with the barn-sale money, he didn't have enough to buy both of them.

"Well, at least you can buy back Granny's binoculars," said Dolores.

"True," said Andy. "But now I'm right back where I started. I don't have a present for Granny's unbirthday."

The shopkeeper was looking out the window. "How do you like that bike?" said the man.

Andy thought about his bike. It was a good bike. He had had it for a long time. But the seat was worn. Springs were popping out, and it was getting uncomfortable. Besides, he and Lucky Duck could walk to places together.

"Would you trade the binoculars case for my bike?" asked Andy.

Dolores gasped. She was used to

seeing Andy on his bike.

"You've got a deal," said the

shopkeeper, holding out his hand.

Andy shook it.

When Andy got home, he hung the binoculars back on the hook in the barn and went upstairs to his room to wrap his present.

4
Unbelievable

This year, the neighbors and Dolores were invited to Andy's barn for the unbirthday party.

Lucky Duck was the official greeter.

They played Pin the Tail on
the Donkey, Musical Chairs, and
Red Light, Green Light. They ate
cupcakes with sprinkles.

Finally it was present time. Dolores

gave Andy and Granny Webb a picture

she had taken of the two of them.

They gave her a jar of raspberry jam.

"Yum!" said Dolores.

Andy Shane opened his present
from Granny. It was a new bike seat
and horn.

Andy looked at Dolores.

Dolores looked at Andy.

"Let's put them on your bike," said

Granny, looking around the barn.

"Open your present first!"

Dolores cried.

Granny Webb opened her present.

It was the binoculars case.

Andy looked at the wall for Granny's binoculars. He wanted to show her how well they fit in the case. But they weren't there.

Granny looked sheepish. "Andy Shane," she said quietly, "I traded my binoculars with Kate at the bicycle shop—for a new bike seat."

Andy laughed. "I traded my bike to the antique dealer for your binoculars case!"

"Wow," said Dolores.

"Wow," said the neighbors.

Andy laughed. "I guess that's what happens when you have an *un*birthday!"

"It is *un*derstandable!" said Granny.

"You'll have to wait *un*til your real

birthday," said Dolores.

"*Un*less," said Andy, who was

already thinking of a plan. . . .

The next day, Andy Shane and
Granny Webb set up an apple stand.
They sold lots of apples.

Then they went to a barn sale.